# THE RELUCTANT DRAGON

Also by Kenneth Grahame and E. H. Shepard

*The Wind in the Willows*

# THE RELUCTANT DRAGON

## Kenneth Grahame

*With original illustrations by E.H. Shepard*

**EGMONT**

# EGMONT

*We bring stories to life*

First published in Great Britain 1995 by Methuen Children's Books
This edition published 2008
by Egmont UK Limited
239 Kensington High Street
London W8 6SA

*The Reluctant Dragon* first appeared in *Dream Days* in 1898
This edition with illustrations by Ernest H. Shepard
first published in 1938 by Holiday House Inc. USA

ISBN 978 1 4052 3729 1

1 3 5 7 9 10 8 6 4 2

A CIP catalogue record for this title is available from the British Library

Typeset by Avon DataSet Ltd, Bidford on Avon, Warwickshire
Printed and bound in Great Britain by the CPI Group

*They knew that book-learning often came in useful at a pinch*

Long ago – might have been hundreds of years ago – in a cottage half-way between an English village and the shoulder of the Downs a shepherd lived with his wife and their little son. Now the shepherd spent his days – and at certain times of the year his nights too – up on the wide ocean-bosom of the Downs, with only the sun and the stars and the sheep for company, and the friendly chattering world of men and women far out of sight and hearing. But his little son, when he wasn't helping his father, and often when he was as well, spent much of his time buried in big volumes that he borrowed from the affable gentry and interested parsons of the country round about. And his parents were very fond of him, and rather proud of him too, though they didn't let on in his hearing, so he was left to go his own way and read as much as he liked; and instead of frequently getting a cuff on the side of the head, as might very well have happened to him, he was treated more or less as an equal by his parents, who sensibly thought it a very fair division of labour that they should supply the practical knowledge, and he the book-learning. They

knew that
book-learning
often came in
useful at a
pinch, in spite
of what their
neighbours said.

*. . . buried in big volumes*

What the Boy chiefly dabbled in was natural
history and fairytales, and he just took them
as they came, in a sandwichy sort of way,
without making any distinctions; and really
his course of reading strikes one as rather
sensible.

One evening the shepherd, who for some
nights past had been disturbed and pre-
occupied, and off his usual mental balance,
came home all of a tremble, and, bursting into

the room where his wife and son were peacefully employed, she with her seam, he in following out the adventures of the Giant with no Heart in his Body, exclaimed with much agitation:

'It's all up with me, Maria! Never no more can I go up on them there Downs, was it ever so!'

'Now don't you take on like that,' said his wife, who was a *very* sensible woman: 'but tell us all about it first, whatever it is as has given you this shake-up, and then me and you and the son here, between us, we ought to be able to get to the bottom of it!'

'It began some nights ago,' said the shepherd. 'You know that cave up there – I never liked it, somehow, and the sheep never liked it neither, and when sheep don't like a thing there's generally some reason for it. Well, for some time past there's been faint noises coming from that cave – noises like heavy sighings, with grunts mixed up in them; and sometimes a snoring, far away down – *real* snoring, yet somehow not *honest* snoring, like you and me o'nights, you know!'

'*I* know,' remarked the Boy quietly.

'Of course I was terrible frightened,' the shepherd went on; 'yet somehow I couldn't keep away. So this very evening, before I come down, I took a cast round by the cave, quietly. And there – O Lord there I saw him at last, as plain as I see you!'

'Saw *who?*' said his wife, beginning to share her husband's nervous terror.

*I saw him at last, as plain as I see you!*

'Why *him*, I'm a-telling you!' said the shepherd. 'He was sticking half-way out of the cave, and seemed to be enjoying of the cool of the evening in a poetical sort of way. He was as big as four cart-horses, and all covered with shiny scales – deep-blue scales at the top of him, shading off to a tender sort o' green below. As he breathed, there was that sort of flicker over his nostrils that you see over our chalk roads on a baking windless day in summer. He had his chin on his paws, and I should say he was meditating about things. Oh, yes, a peaceable sort o' beast enough, and not ramping or carrying on or doing anything but what was quite right and proper. I admit all that. And yet, what am I to do? *Scales*, you know, and claws, and a tail for certain, though I didn't see that end of him – I ain't *used* to 'em, and I don't *hold* with 'em, and that's a fact!'

The Boy, who had apparently been absorbed in his book during his father's recital, now closed the volume, yawned, clasped his hands behind his head, and said sleepily:

'It's all right, Father. Don't you worry. It's only a dragon.'

'Only a dragon?' cried his father. 'What do you mean, sitting there, you and your dragons? *Only* a dragon indeed! And what do *you* know about it?'

"Cos it *is,* and 'cos I *do* know,' replied the Boy, quietly. 'Look here, Father, you know we've each of us got our line. *You* know about sheep, and weather, and things; *I* know about dragons. I always said, you know, that that cave up there was a dragon-cave. I always said it must have belonged to a dragon some time, and ought to belong to a dragon now, if rules count for anything. Well, now you tell me it *has* got a dragon, and so *that's* all right. I'm not half as much surprised as when you told

8

me it *hadn't* got a dragon. Rules always come right if you wait quietly. Now, please, just leave this all to me. And I'll stroll up to-morrow morning – no, in the morning I can't, I've got a whole heap of things to do – well, perhaps in the evening, if I'm quite free, I'll go up and have a talk to him, and you'll find it'll be all right. Only, please, don't you go worrying round there without me. You don't understand 'em a bit, and they're very sensitive, you know!'

'He's quite right, Father,' said the sensible mother. 'As he says, dragons is his line and not ours. He's wonderful knowing about book-beasts, as every one allows. And to tell the truth, I'm not half happy in my own mind, thinking of that poor animal lying alone up there, without a bit o' hot supper or anyone to change the news with; and maybe we'll be able to do something for him; and if he ain't quite respectable our Boy'll find it out quick enough. He's got a pleasant sort o' way with him that makes everybody tell him everything.'

Next day, after he'd had his tea, the Boy strolled up the chalky track that led to the summit of the Downs; and there, sure enough, he found the dragon, stretched lazily on the sward in front of his cave. The view from that point was a magnificent one. To the right and left, the bare and billowy leagues of Downs; in front, the vale, with its clustered homesteads, its threads of white roads running through orchards and well-tilled acreage, and, far away, a hint of grey old cities on the horizon. A cool breeze played over the surface of the grass and the silver shoulder of a large moon was showing above distant junipers. No wonder the dragon seemed in a peaceful and contented mood; indeed, as the Boy approached he could hear the beast purring with a happy regularity. 'Well, we live and learn!' he said to himself. 'None of my books ever told me that dragons purred!'

'Hullo, dragon!' said the Boy, quietly, when he had got up to him.

The dragon, on hearing the approaching footsteps, made the beginning of a courteous effort to rise. But when he saw it was a Boy, he set his eyebrows severely.

'Now don't you hit me,' he said; 'or bung

stones, or squirt water, or anything. I won't have it, I tell you!'

'Not goin' to hit you,' said the Boy wearily, dropping on the grass beside the beast: 'and don't, for goodness' sake, keep on saying "Don't"; I hear so much of it, and it's monotonous, and makes me tired. I've simply looked in to ask you how you were and all that sort of thing; but if I'm in the way I can easily clear out. I've lots of friends, and no one can say I'm in the habit of shoving myself in where I'm not wanted!'

'No, no, don't go off in a huff,' said the dragon, hastily; 'fact is, I'm as happy up here as the day's long; never without an occupation, dear fellow, never without an occupation! And yet, between ourselves, it *is* a trifle dull at times.'

The Boy bit off a stalk of grass and chewed it. 'Going to make a long stay here?' he asked, politely.

'Can't hardly say at present,' replied the dragon. 'It seems a nice place enough – but I've only been here a short time, and one must look about and reflect and consider before settling down. It's rather a serious thing, settling down. Besides – now I'm going to tell you something! You'd never guess it if you tried ever so! – fact is, I'm such a confoundedly lazy beggar!'

'You surprise me,' said the Boy, civilly.

'It's the sad truth,' the dragon went on, settling down between his paws and evidently delighted to have found a listener at last; 'and I fancy that's really how I came to be here. You see all the other fellows were so active and *earnest* and all that sort of thing – always rampaging, and skirmishing, and scouring the desert sands, and pacing the margin of the sea, and chasing knights all over the place, and devouring damsels, and going on generally – whereas I liked to get my meals regular and then to prop my back against a bit of rock and snooze a bit, and wake up and think of things going on and how they kept going on just the same, you know! So when it happened I got fairly caught.'

'When *what* happened, please?' asked the Boy.

'That's just what I don't precisely know,' said the dragon. 'I suppose the earth sneezed, or shook itself, or the bottom dropped out of something. Anyhow there was a shake and a roar and a general stramash, and I found myself miles away underground and wedged in as tight as tight. Well, thank goodness, my wants are few, and at any rate I had peace and quietness and wasn't always being asked to come along and *do* something. And I've got such an active mind – always occupied, I assure you! But time went on, and there was a certain sameness about the life, and at last I began to think it would be fun to work my way upstairs and see what you other fellows were doing. So I scratched and burrowed, and worked this way and that way and at last I came out through this cave here. And I like the country, and the view, and the people – what I've seen of 'em – and on the whole I feel inclined to settle down here.'

'What's your mind always occupied about?' asked the Boy. 'That's what I want to know.'

The dragon coloured slightly and looked away. Presently he said bashfully:

'Did you ever – just for fun – try to make

up poetry – verses, you know?'

''Course I have,' said the Boy. 'Heaps of it. And some of it's quite good, I feel sure, only there's no one here cares about it. Mother's very kind and all that, when I read it to her, and so's Father for that matter. But somehow they don't seem to –'

'Exactly,' cried the dragon; 'my own case exactly. They don't seem to, and you can't argue with 'em about it. Now you've got culture, you have, I could tell it on you at once, and I should just like your candid opinion about some little things I threw off lightly, when I was down there. I'm awfully pleased to have met you, and I'm hoping the other neighbours will be equally agreeable. There was a very nice old gentleman up here only last night, but he didn't seem to want to intrude.'

'That was my father,' said the Boy, 'and he *is* a nice old gentleman, and I'll introduce you some day if you like.'

'Can't you two come up here and dine or something to-morrow?' asked the dragon, eagerly. 'Only, of course, if you've got nothing better to do,' he added politely.

'Thanks awfully,' said the Boy, 'but we don't go out anywhere without my mother, and, to tell you the truth, I'm afraid she mightn't quite approve of you. You see there's no getting over the hard fact that you're a dragon, is there? And when you talk of settling down, and the neighbours, and so on, I can't help feeling that you don't quite realise your position. You're an enemy of the human race, you see!'

'Haven't got an enemy in the world,' said the dragon, cheerfully. 'Too lazy to make 'em, to begin with. And if I *do* read other fellows my poetry, I'm always ready to listen to theirs!'

'Oh, dear!' cried the Boy. 'I wish you'd try and grasp the situation properly. When the other people find you out, they'll come after you with spears and swords and all sorts of things. You'll have to be exterminated, according to their way of looking at it! You're a scourge, and a pest, and a baneful monster!'

'Not a word of truth in it,' said the dragon, wagging his head solemnly. 'Character'll bear the strictest investigation. And now, there's a

*Not a word of truth in it*

little sonnet-thing I was working on when you appeared on the scene –'

'Oh, if you *won't* be sensible,' cried the Boy, getting up, 'I'm going off home. No, I can't stop for sonnets; my mother's sitting up. I'll look you up to-morrow, sometime or other, and do for goodness' sake try and realise that you're a pestilential scourge, or you'll find yourself in a most awful fix. Good-night!'

The Boy found it an easy matter to set the mind of his parents at ease about his new friend. They had always left that branch to him, and they took his word without a murmur. The shepherd was formally introduced and many compliments and kind inquiries were exchanged. His wife, however, though expressing her willingness to do anything she could – to mend things, or set the cave to rights, or cook a little something when the dragon had been poring over sonnets and forgotten his meals, as male things *will* do, could not be brought to recognise him formally. The fact that he was a dragon and 'they didn't know who he was' seemed to count for everything with her. She made no objection, however, to her little son spending his evenings with the dragon quietly, so long as he was home by nine o'clock; and many a pleasant night they had, sitting on the sward, while the dragon told stories of old, old times, when dragons were quite plentiful and the world was a livelier place than it is now, and life was full of thrills and jumps and surprises.

What the Boy had feared, however, soon
came to pass. The most modest and retiring
dragon in the world, if he's as big as four cart-
horses and covered with blue scales, cannot
keep altogether out of the public view. And so
in the village tavern of nights the fact that a
real live dragon sat brooding in the cave on the
Downs was naturally a subject for talk. Though
the villagers were extremely frightened, they
were rather proud as well. It was a distinction
to have a dragon of your own, and it was felt to
be a feather in the cap of the village. Still, all
were agreed that this sort of thing couldn't be
allowed to go on. The dreadful beast must be
exterminated, the country-side must be freed
from this pest, this terror, this destroying
scourge. The fact that not even a hen-roost was

the worse for the dragon's arrival wasn't allowed to have anything to do with it. He was a dragon, and he couldn't deny it, and if he didn't choose to behave as such that was his own lookout. But in spite of much valiant talk no hero was found willing to take sword and spear and free the suffering village and win deathless fame; and each night's heated discussion always ended in nothing. Meanwhile the dragon, a happy Bohemian, lolled on the turf, enjoyed the sunsets, told antediluvian anecdotes to the Boy, and polished his old verses while meditating on fresh ones.

One day the Boy, on walking in to the village, found everything wearing a festal appearance which was not to be accounted for in the calendar. Carpets and gay-coloured stuffs were hung out of the windows, the church-bells clamoured noisily, the little street was flower-strewn, and the whole population jostled each other along either side of it, chattering, shoving, and ordering each other to stand back. The Boy saw a friend of his own age in the crowd and hailed him.

'What's up?' he cried. 'Is it the players, or bears, or a circus, or what?'

'It's all right,' his friend hailed back. 'He's a-coming.'

'*Who's* a-coming?' demanded the Boy, thrusting into the throng.

'Why, St George, of course,' replied his friend. 'He's heard tell of our dragon, and he's

*. . . won't there be a
jolly fight!*

comin' on purpose to slay the deadly beast,
and free us from his horrid yoke. O my! won't
there be a jolly fight!'

Here was news indeed! The Boy felt that
he ought to make quite sure for himself, and
he wriggled himself in between the legs of his
good-natured elders, abusing them all the

time for their unmannerly habit of shoving. Once in the front rank, he breathlessly awaited the arrival.

Presently from the far-away end of the line came the sound of cheering. Next, the measured tramp of a great war-horse made his heart beat quicker, and then he found himself cheering with the rest, as, amidst welcoming shouts, shrill cries of women, uplifting of babies and waving of hand-kerchiefs, St George paced slowly up the street. The Boy's heart stood still and he breathed with sobs, the beauty and the grace of the hero were so far beyond anything he had yet seen. His fluted armour was inlaid with gold, his plumed helmet hung at his saddle-bow, and his thick fair hair framed a face gracious and gentle beyond expression till you caught the sternness in his eyes. He drew rein in front of the little inn, and the villagers crowded round with greetings and thanks and voluble statements of their wrongs and grievances and oppressions. The Boy heard the grave gentle voice of the Saint, assuring them that all would be well now, and that he would stand by them and see them righted and free them from their foe; then he dismounted and passed through the doorway and the crowd poured in after him. But the Boy made off up the hill as fast as he could lay his legs to the ground.

'It's all up, dragon!' he shouted as soon as he was within sight of the beast. 'He's coming! He's here now! You'll have to pull yourself together and *do* something at last!'

*It's all up, dragon!*

The dragon was licking his scales and
rubbing them with a bit of house-flannel the
Boy's mother had lent him, till he shone like
a great turquoise.

'Don't be *violent*, Boy,' he said without
looking round. 'Sit down and get your breath,

and try and remember that the noun governs the verb, and then perhaps you'll be good enough to tell me *who's* coming?'

'That's right, take it coolly,' said the Boy. 'Hope you'll be half as cool when I've got through with my news. It's only St George who's coming, that's all; he rode into the village half-an-hour ago. Of course you can lick him – a great big fellow like you! But I thought I'd warn you, 'cos he's sure to be round early, and he's got the longest, wickedest-looking spear you ever did see!' And the Boy got up and began to jump round in sheer delight at the prospect of the battle.

'O deary, deary me,' moaned the dragon; 'this is too awful. I won't see him, and that's flat. I don't want to know the fellow at all. I'm sure he's not nice. You must tell him to go away at once, please. Say he can write if he likes, but I can't give him an interview. I'm not seeing anybody at present.'

'Now dragon, dragon,' said the Boy imploringly, 'don't be perverse and wrong-headed. You've got to fight him some time or other, you know, 'cos he's St George and you're the dragon. Better get it over, and then we can go on with the sonnets. And you ought to consider other people a little, too. If it's been dull up here for you, think how dull it's been for me!'

'My dear little man,' said the dragon solemnly, 'just understand, once for all, that I can't fight and I won't fight. I've never fought in my life, and I'm not going to begin now, just to give you a Roman holiday. In old days I always let the other fellows – the *earnest* fellow – do all the fighting, and no doubt that's why I have the pleasure of being here now.'

'But if you don't fight he'll cut your head off!' gasped the Boy, miserable at the prospect of losing both his fight and his friend.

'Oh, I think not,' said the dragon in his lazy way. 'You'll be able to arrange something. I've every confidence in you, you're such a *manager*. Just run down, there's a dear chap, and make it all right. I leave it entirely to you.'

The Boy made his way back to the village in a state of great despondency. First of all, there wasn't going to be any fight; next, his dear and honoured friend the dragon hadn't shown up in quite such a heroic light as he would have liked; and lastly, whether the dragon was a hero at heart or not, it made no difference, for St George would most undoubtedly cut his head off. 'Arrange things indeed!' he said bitterly to himself. 'The dragon treats the whole affair as if it was an invitation to tea and croquet.'

The villagers were straggling homewards as he passed up the street, all of them in the highest spirits, and gleefully discussing the splendid fight that was in store. The Boy pursued his way to the inn, and passed into the principal chamber, where St George now sat alone, musing over the chances of the fight, and the sad stories of rapine and of wrong that had so lately been poured into his sympathetic ears.

*May I come in, St George?*

'May I come in, St George?' said the Boy
politely, as he paused at the door. 'I want to
talk to you about this little matter of the

dragon, if you're not tired of it by this time.'

'Yes, come in, Boy,' said the Saint kindly. 'Another tale of misery and wrong, I fear me. Is it a kind parent, then, of whom the tyrant has bereft you? Or some tender sister or brother? Well, it shall soon be avenged.'

'Nothing of the sort,' said the Boy. 'There's a misunderstanding somewhere, and I want to put it right. The fact is, this is a *good* dragon.'

'Exactly,' said St George, smiling pleasantly, 'I quite understand. A good *dragon*. Believe me, I do not in the least regret that he is an adversary worthy of my steel, and no feeble specimen of his noxious tribe.'

'But he's *not* a noxious tribe,' cried the Boy distressedly. 'Oh dear, oh dear, how *stupid* men are when they get an idea into their heads! I tell you he's a *good* dragon, and a friend of mine, and tells me the most beautiful stories you ever heard, all about old times and when he was little. And he's been so kind to Mother, and Mother'd do anything for him. And Father likes him too, though Father doesn't hold with art and poetry much, and always falls asleep when the dragon starts talking about *style*. But the fact is, nobody can help liking him when once they know him. He's so engaging and so trustful, and as simple as a child!'

'Sit down, and draw your chair up,' said St George. 'I like a fellow who sticks up for his friends, and I'm sure the dragon has his good points, if he's got a friend like you. But that's

*. . . listening to tales of murder*

not the question. All this evening I've been
listening, with grief and anguish unspeakable,
to tales of murder, theft, and wrong; rather
too highly coloured, perhaps, not always
quite convincing, but forming in the main a

most serious roll of crime. History teaches us that the greatest rascals often possess all the domestic virtues; and I fear that your cultivated friend, in spite of the qualities which have won (and rightly) your regard, has got to be speedily exterminated.'

'Oh, you've been taking in all the yarns those fellows have been telling you,' said the Boy impatiently. 'Why, our villagers are the biggest storytellers in all the country round. It's a known fact. You're a stranger in these parts, or else you'd have heard it already. All they want is a *fight*. They're the most awful beggars for getting up fights – it's meat and drink to them. Dogs, bulls, dragons – anything so long as it's a fight. Why, they've got a poor innocent badger in the stable behind here, at this moment. They were going to have some fun with him to-day, but they're saving him up now till *your* little affair's over. And I've no doubt they've been telling you what a hero you were, and how you were bound to win, in the cause of right and justice, and so on; but let me tell you, I came down the street just now, and they were betting six to four on the dragon freely!'

'Six to four on the dragon!' murmured St George sadly, resting his cheek on his hand. 'This is an evil world, and sometimes I begin to think that all the wickedness in it is not entirely bottled up inside the dragons. And yet – may not this wily beast have misled you as to his real character, in order that your good report of him may serve as a cloak for his evil deeds? Nay, may there not be, at this very moment, some hapless Princess mmured within yonder gloomy cavern?'

The moment he had spoken, St George was sorry for what he had said, the Boy looked so genuinely distressed.

'I assure you, St George,' he said earnestly, 'there's nothing of the sort in the cave at all. The dragon's a real gentleman, every inch of him, and I may say that no one would be more shocked and grieved than he would, at hearing you talk in that – that *loose* way about matters on which he has very strong views!'

'Well, perhaps I've been over-credulous,' said St George. 'Perhaps I've misjudged the animal. But what are we to do? Here are the dragon and I, almost face to face, each supposed to be thirsting for each other's blood. I don't see any way out of it, exactly. What do you suggest? Can't you arrange things, somehow?'

'That's just what the dragon said,' replied the Boy, rather nettled. 'Really, the way you two seem to leave everything to me – I suppose you couldn't be persuaded to go away quietly, could you?'

'Impossible, I fear,' said the Saint. 'Quite against the rules. *You* know that as well as I do.'

'Well, then, look here,' said the Boy, 'it's early yet – would you mind strolling up with me and seeing the dragon and talking it over? It's not far, and any friend of mine will be most welcome.'

'Well, it's *irregular*,' said St George, rising,

'but really it seems about the most sensible thing to do. You're taking a lot of trouble on your friend's account,' he added, good-naturedly, as they passed out through the door together. 'But cheer up! Perhaps there won't have to be any fight after all.'

'Oh, but I hope there will, though!' replied the little fellow, wistfully.

'I've brought a friend to see you, dragon,' said the Boy, rather loud.

The dragon woke up with a start. 'I was just – er – thinking about things,' he said in his simple way. 'Very pleased to make your acquaintance, sir. Charming weather we're having!'

'This is St George,' said the Boy, shortly. 'St George, let me introduce you to the dragon. We've come up to talk things over quitely, dragon, and now for goodness' sake do let us have a little straight common-sense, and come to some practical business-like arrangement, for I'm sick of views and theories of life and personal tendencies, and

*I've brought a friend to see you*

all that sort of thing. I may perhaps add that my mother's sitting up.'

'So glad to meet you, St George,' began the dragon rather nervously, 'because you've been a great traveller, I hear, and I've always been rather a stay-at-home. But I can show you many antiquities, many interesting features of our country-side, if you're stopping here any time –'

'I think,' said St George, in his frank, pleasant way, 'that we'd really better take the advice of our young friend here, and try to come to some understanding, on a business footing, about this little affair of ours. Now don't you think that after all the simplest plan would be just to fight it out, according to the rules, and let the best man win? They're betting on you, I may tell you, down in the village, but I don't mind that!'

'Oh, yes, *do*, dragon,' said the Boy, delightedly; 'it'll save such a lot of bother!'

'My young friend, you shut up,' said the dragon severely. 'Believe me, St George,' he went on, 'there's nobody in the world I'd sooner oblige than you and this young gentleman here. But the whole thing's nonsense, and conventionality, and popular thickheadedness. There's absolutely nothing to fight about, from beginning to end. And anyhow I'm not going to, so that settles it!'

'But supposing I make you?' said St George, rather nettled.

'You can't,' said the dragon, triumphantly.

'I should only go into my cave and retire for a time down the hole I came up. You'd soon get heartily sick of sitting outside and waiting for me to come out and fight you. And as soon as you'd really gone away, why, I'd come up again gaily, for I tell you frankly, I like this place, and I'm going to stay here!'

St George gazed for a while on the fair landscape around them. 'But this would be a beautiful place for a fight,' he began again persuasively. 'These great bare rolling Downs for the arena – and me in my golden armour showing up against your big blue scaly coils! Think what a picture it would make!'

'Now you're trying to get at me through my artistic sensibilities,' said the dragon. 'But it won't work. Not but what it would make a very pretty picture, as you say,' he added, wavering a little.

'We seem to be getting nearer to *business*,' put in the Boy. 'You must see, dragon, that there's got to be a fight of some sort, 'cos you can't want to have to go down that dirty old hole again and stop there till goodness knows when.'

'It might be arranged,' said St George, thoughtfully. 'I *must* spear you somewhere, of course, but I'm not bound to hurt you very much. There's such a lot of you that there must be a few *spare* places somewhere. Here, for instance, just behind your foreleg. It couldn't hurt you much, just here!'

'Now you're tickling, George,' said the dragon, coyly. 'No, that place won't do at all.

*Now you're tickling,
George*

Even if it didn't hurt – and I'm sure it would,
awfully – it would make me laugh, and that
would spoil everything.'

'Let's try somewhere else then,' said St
George, patiently. 'Under your neck, for

instance – all these folds of thick skin – if I speared you here you'd never even know I'd done it!'

'Yes, but are you sure you can hit off the right place?' asked the dragon, anxiously.

'Of course I am,' said St George, with confidence. 'You leave that to me!'

'It's just because I've *got* to leave it to you that I'm asking,' replied the dragon, rather testily. 'No doubt you would deeply regret any error you might make in the hurry of the moment; but you wouldn't regret it half as much as I should! However, I suppose we've got to trust somebody, as we go through life, and your plan seems, on the whole, as good a one as any.'

'Look here, dragon,' interrupted the Boy, a

little jealous on behalf of his friend, who seemed to be getting all the worst of the bargain: 'I don't quite see where *you* come in! There's to be a fight, apparently, and you're to be licked; and what I want to know is, what are *you* going to get out of it?'

'St George,' said the dragon, 'just tell him, please – what will happen after I'm vanquished in the deadly combat?'

'Well, according to the rules I suppose I shall lead you in triumph down to the market-place or whatever answers to it,' said St George.

'Precisely,' said the dragon. 'And then –'

'And then there'll be shoutings and speeches and things,' continued St George. 'And I shall explain that you're converted, and see the error of your ways, and so on.'

'Quite so,' said the dragon. 'And then –?'

'Oh, and then –' said St George, 'why, and then there will be the usual banquet, I suppose.'

'Exactly,' said the dragon; 'and that's where *I* come in. Look here,' he continued, addressing the Boy, 'I'm bored to death up here, and no one really appreciates me. I'm going into Society, I am, through the kindly aid of our friend here, who's taking such a lot of trouble on my account; and you'll find I've got all the qualities to endear me to people who entertain! So now that's all settled, and if you don't mind – I'm an old-fashioned fellow – don't want to turn you out, but –'

'Remember, you'll have to do your proper share of the fighting, dragon!' said St George, as he took the hint and rose to go; 'I mean ramping, and breathing fire, and so on!'

'I can *ramp* all right,' replied the dragon, confidently; 'as to breathing fire, it's surprising how easily one gets out of practice; but I'll do the best I can. Goodnight!'

They had descended the hill and were almost back in the village again, when St George stopped short. '*Knew* I had forgotten something,' he said. 'There ought to be a Princess. Terror-stricken and chained to a rock, and all that sort of thing. Boy, can't you arrange a Princess?'

The Boy was in the middle of a tremendous yawn. 'I'm tired to death,' he wailed, 'and I *can't* arrange a Princess, or anything more, at this time of night. And my mother's sitting up, and *do* stop asking me to arrange more things till tomorrow!'

Next morning the people began streaming up to the Downs at quite an early hour, in their Sunday clothes and carrying baskets with bottlenecks sticking out of them, every one intent on securing good places for the combat. This was not exactly a simple matter, for of course it was quite possible that the dragon might win, and in that case even those who had put their money on him felt they could hardly expect him to deal with his backers on a different footing to the rest. Places were chosen, therefore, with circum-spection and with a view to a speedy retreat in case of emergency; and the front rank was mostly composed of boys who had escaped

*Places were chosen with
circumspection*

from parental control and now sprawled and rolled about on the grass, regardless of the shrill threats and warnings discharged at them by their anxious mothers behind.

The Boy had secured a good front place, well up towards the cave, and was feeling as anxious as a stage-manager on a first night. Could the dragon be depended upon? He might change his mind and vote the whole performance rot; or else, seeing that the affair had been so hastily planned, without even a rehearsal, he might be too nervous to show up. The Boy looked narrowly at the cave, but it showed no sign of life or occupation. Could the dragon have made a moon-light flitting?

The higher portions of the ground were now black with sightseers, and presently a sound of cheering and a waving of handkerchiefs told that something was visible to them which the Boy, far up towards the dragon-end of the line as he was, could not yet see. A minute more and St George's red plumes topped the hill, as the Saint rode slowly forth on the great level space which stretched up to the grim mouth of the cave. Very gallant and beautiful he looked, on his tall war-horse, his golden armour glancing in the sun, his great spear held erect, the little white pennon, crimson-crossed, fluttering at its point. He drew rein and remained motionless. The lines of spectators began to give back a little, nervously; and even the boys in front stopped pulling hair and cuffing each other, and leaned forward expectant.

'Now then, dragon!' muttered the Boy impatiently, fidgeting where he sat. He need not have distressed himself, had he only known. The dramatic possibilities of the thing had tickled the dragon immensely, and he had been up from an early hour, preparing for his first public appearance with as much heartiness as if the years had run backwards, and he had been again a little dragonlet, playing with his sisters on the floor of their mother's cave, at the game of saints-and-dragons, in which the dragon was bound to win.

A low muttering, mingled with snorts, now made itself heard; rising to a bellowing roar that seemed to fill the plain. Then a cloud of smoke obscured the mouth of the cave, and out of the midst of it the dragon himself, shining, sea-blue, magnificent, pranced splendidly forth; and everybody said, 'Oo-oo-oo!' as if he had been a mighty rocket! His scales were glittering, his long spiky tail lashed his sides, his claws tore up the turf and sent it flying high over his back, and smoke and fire incessantly jetted from his angry nostrils. 'Oh, well done, dragon!' cried the Boy, excitedly. 'Didn't think he had it in him!' he added to himself.

*. . . everybody said, 'Oo-oo-oo!'*

St George lowered his spear, bent his
head, dug his heels into his horse's sides, and
came thundering over the turf. The dragon
charged with a roar and a squeal – a great
blue whirling combination of coils and snorts

and clashing jaws and spikes and fire.

'Missed!' yelled the crowd. There was a moment's entanglement of golden armour and blue-green coils, and spiky tail, and then the great horse, tearing at his bit, carried the Saint, his spear swung high in the air, almost up to the mouth of the cave.

The dragon sat down and barked viciously, while St George with difficulty pulled his horse round into position.

'End of Round One!' thought the Boy. 'How well they managed it! But I hope the Saint won't get excited. I can trust the dragon all right. What a regular play-actor the fellow is!'

St George had at last prevailed on his horse to stand steady, and was looking round him as he wiped his brow. Catching sight of the Boy, he smiled and nodded, and held up three fingers for an instant.

'It seems to be all planned out,' said the Boy to himself. 'Round Three is to be the finishing one, evidently. Wish it could have lasted a bit longer. Whatever's that old fool of a dragon up to now?'

The dragon was employing the interval in giving a ramping-performance for the benefit of the crowd. Ramping, it should be explained, consists in running round and round in a wide circle, and sending waves and ripples of movement along the whole length of your spine, from your pointed ears right down to the spike at the end of your long tail. When you are covered with blue scales, the effect is particularly pleasing; and the Boy recollected the dragon's recently expressed wish to become a social success.

St George now gathered up his reins and began to move forward, dropping the point of his spear and settling himself firmly in the saddle.

'Time!' yelled everybody excitedly; and the dragon, leaving off his ramping, sat up on end, and began to leap from one side to the other with huge ungainly bounds, whooping like a Red Indian. This naturally disconcerted the horse, who swerved violently, the Saint only just saving himself by the mane; and as they shot past the dragon delivered a vicious snap at the horse's tail which sent the poor beast careering madly far over the Downs, so that the language of the Saint, who had lost a stirrup, was fortunately inaudible to the general assemblage.

Round Two evoked audible evidence of friendly feeling towards the dragon. The spectators were not slow to appreciate a combatant who could hold his own so well and clearly wanted to show good sport; and many encouraging remarks reached the ears of our friend as he strutted to and fro, his chest thrust out and his tail in the air, hugely enjoying his new popularity.

St George had dismounted and was tightening his girths, and telling his horse, with quite an Oriental flow of imagery, exactly what he thought of him, and his relations, and his conduct on the present occasion; so the Boy made his way down to the Saint's end of the line, and held his spear for him.

'It's been a jolly fight, St George!' he said with a sigh. 'Can't you let it last a bit longer?'

'Well, I think I'd better not,' replied the Saint. 'The fact is, your simple-minded old friend's getting conceited, now they've begun cheering him, and he'll forget all about the arrangement and take to playing the fool, and there's no telling where he would stop. I'll just finish him off this round.'

He swung himself into the saddle and took his spear from the Boy. 'Now don't you be afraid,' he added kindly. 'I've marked my spot exactly, and *he's* sure to give me all the assistance in his power, because he knows it's his only chance of being asked to the banquet!'

St George now shortened his spear, bringing the butt well up under his arm; and, instead of galloping as before, trotted smartly towards the dragon, who crouched at his approach, flicking his tail till it cracked in the air like a great cart-whip. The Saint wheeled as he neared his opponent and circled warily round him, keeping his eye on the spare place; while the dragon, adopting similar tactics, paced with caution round the same circle, occasionally feinting with his head. So the two sparred for an opening, while the spectators maintained a breathless silence.

Though the round lasted for some minutes, the end was so swift that all the Boy saw was a lightning movement of the Saint's arm, and then a whirl and a confusion of

... *winked solemnly*

spines, claws, tail, and flying bits of turf. The dust cleared away, the spectators whooped and ran in cheering, and the Boy made out that the dragon was down, pinned to the earth by the spear, while St George had dismounted, and stood astride of him.

It all seemed so genuine that the Boy ran in breathlessly, hoping the dear old dragon wasn't really hurt. As he approached, the dragon lifted one large eyelid, winked solemnly, and collapsed again. He was held fast to earth by the neck, but the Saint had hit him in the spare place agreed upon, and it didn't even seem to tickle.

'Bain't you goin' to cut 'is 'ed orf, master?' asked one of the applauding crowd. He had backed the dragon, and naturally felt a trifle sore.

'Well, not *to-day*, I think,' replied St George, pleasantly. 'You see, that can be done *any* time. There's no hurry at all. I think we'll all go down to the village first, and have some

refreshment, and then I'll give him a good talking-to, and you'll find he'll be a very different dragon!'

At that magic word *refreshment* the whole crowd formed up in procession and silently awaited the signal to start. The time for talking and cheering and betting was past, the hour for action had arrived. St George, hauling on his spear with both hands, released the dragon, who rose and shook himself and ran his eye over his spikes and

*Then the Saint led off
the procession*

scales and things, to see that they were all in order. Then the Saint mounted and led off the procession, the dragon following meekly in the company of the Boy, while the thirsty spectators kept at a respectful interval behind.

There were great doings when they got down to the village again, and had formed up in front of the inn. After refreshment St George made a speech, in which he informed his audience that he had removed their direful scourge, at a great deal of trouble and inconvenience to himself, and now they weren't to go about grumbling and fancying they'd got grievances, because they hadn't. And they shouldn't be so fond of fights, because next time they might have to do the fighting themselves, which would not be the same thing at all. And there was a certain badger in the inn stables which had got to be released at once, and he'd come and see it done himself. Then he told them that the dragon had been thinking things over, and saw that there were two sides to every question, and he wasn't going to do it any more, and if they were good perhaps he'd stay and settle down there. So they must make friends, and not be prejudiced, and go about fancying they knew everything there was to be known, because they didn't, not by a long way. And he warned them against the sin of romancing, and making up stories and fancying other people would believe them just because they were plausible and highly-coloured. Then he sat down, amidst much repentant cheering, and the dragon nudged the Boy in the ribs and whispered that he couldn't have done it better himself. Then everyone went off to get ready for the banquet.

Banquets are always pleasant things, consisting mostly, as they do, of eating and drinking; but the specially nice thing about a banquet is that it comes when something's over, and there's nothing more to worry about, and to-morrow seems a long way off. St George was happy because there had been a fight and he hadn't had to kill anybody; for he didn't really like killing, though he generally had to do it. The dragon was happy because there had been a fight, and so far from being hurt in it he had won popularity and a sure footing in society. The Boy was happy because there had been a fight, and in spite of it all his two friends were on the best of terms. And all the others were happy because there had been a fight, and – well, they didn't require any other reasons for their happiness. The dragon exerted himself to say the right thing to everybody, and proved the life and soul of the evening; while the Saint and the Boy, as they looked on, felt that they were only assisting at a feast of which the honour and the glory were entirely the dragon's. But they didn't mind that, being good fellows, and the dragon was not in the least proud or forgetful. On the contrary, every ten minutes or so he leant over towards the Boy and said impressively: 'Look here! you *will* see me home afterwards, won't you?' And the Boy always nodded, though he had promised his mother not to be out late.

At last the banquet was over, the guests had dropped away with many good-nights and congratulations and invitations, and the dragon, who had seen the last of them off the premises, emerged into the street followed by the Boy, wiped his brow, sighed, sat down in the road and gazed at the stars. 'Jolly night it's been!' he murmured. 'Jolly stars! Jolly little place this! Think I shall just stop here. Don't feel like climbing up any beastly hill. Boy's promised to see me home. Boy had better do it then! No responsibility on my part. Responsibility all Boy's!' And his chin sank on his broad chest and he slumbered peacefully.

'Oh, *get* up, dragon,' cried the Boy, piteously. 'You *know* my mother's sitting up, and I'm so tired, and you made me promise to see you home, and I never knew what it meant or I wouldn't have done it!' And the Boy sat down in the road by the side of the sleeping dragon, and cried.

The door behind them opened, a stream of light illumined the road, and St George, who had come out for a stroll in the cool night-air, caught sight of the two figures sitting there – the great motionless dragon and the tearful little Boy.

'What's the matter, Boy?' he inquired kindly, stepping to his side.

'Oh, it's this great lumbering *pig* of a

dragon!' sobbed the Boy. 'First he makes me promise to see him home, and then he says I'd better do it, and goes to sleep! Might as well try to see a *haystack* home! And I'm so tired, and Mother's –' here he broke down again.

'Now don't take on,' said St George. 'I'll stand by you, and we'll *both* see him home. Wake up, dragon!' he said sharply, shaking the beast by the elbow.

The dragon looked up sleepily. 'What a night, George!' he murmured; 'what a –'

'Now look here, dragon,' said the Saint, firmly. 'Here's this little fellow waiting to see you home, and you *know* he ought to have been in bed these two hours, and what his mother'll say *I* don't know, and anybody but a selfish pig would have *made* him go to bed long ago –'

'And he *shall* go to bed!' cried the dragon, starting up. 'Poor little chap, only fancy his being up at this hour! It's a shame, that's what it is, and I don't think, St George, you've been very considerate – but come along at once, and don't let us have any more arguing or shilly-shallying. You give me hold of your hand, Boy – thank you, George, an arm up the hill is just what I wanted!'

So they set off up the hill arm-in-arm, the Saint, the Dragon, and the Boy. The lights in the little village began to go out; but there were stars, and a late moon, as they climbed to the Downs together. And, as they turned the last corner and disappeared from view,

*. . . snatches of an old song*

snatches of an old song were borne back on the night-breeze. I can't be certain which of them was singing, but I *think* it was the Dragon!

Also by Kenneth Grahame and
illustrated by E. H. Shepard

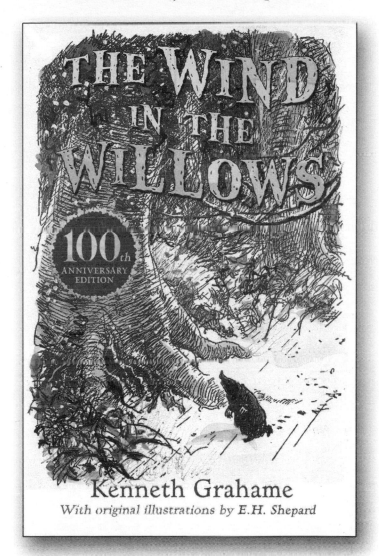

# The Wind in the Willows

A classic tale of animal friendship, messing
about in boats and speeding in motor cars!

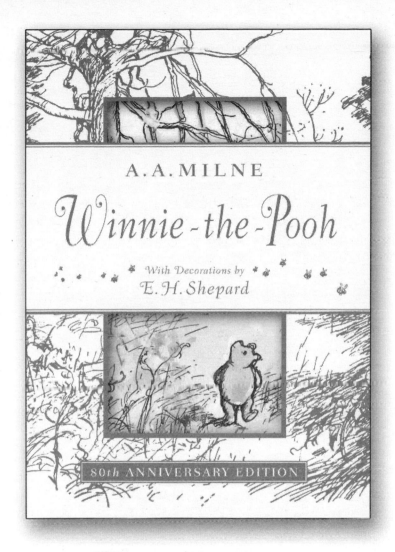

# Winnie-the-Pooh

By A A Milne,
illustrated by E. H. Shepard

Join Pooh and his friends in their adventures in the 100 Acre Wood.
Classic stories loved by generations of children.

# Tumtum and Nutmeg

By Emily Bearn,
illustrated by Nick Price

A tale of two mice and one plan to get rid of them. Can
Tumtum and Nutmeg foil Aunt Ivy's plot?
A beautifully written story, destined to become a future classic.

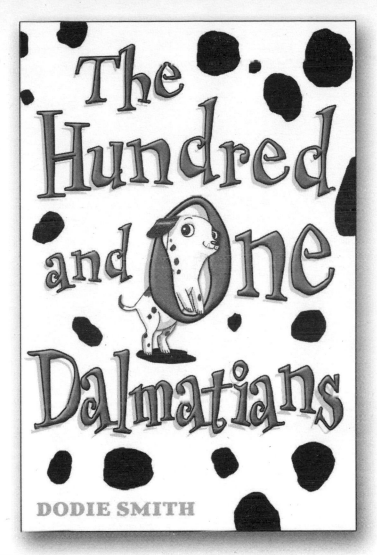

# The Hundred and One Dalmatians

By Dodie Smith,
illustrated by David Roberts

Missus and Pongo's pups have been stolen by the evil
Cruella de Vil! Can the dogs rescue them?